Pirates Ahoy

Ghost of Pebble Rock

ISBN: 9780645350760

Also by Brian Dry

The Last Dragon's egg
Ghost of Pebble Rock
Pirates Ahoy (Ghost of Pebble Rock)

Into the Darkness
'Bang-bang
Mr Yellowfoot's
Treeware
Pirates Ahoy me hearty's
'Test
'Pickle the stew
In the beginning
Six weeks passed...
The Word is Believe
Queen of the Banshees
The End.
If you enjoyed this story

Into the Darkness

(The haunting)

Three wise cats clawed at a toadstool and meowed, "wake-up, wake-up!"

Hannah wiped the sticky crumbs from her mind and opened one eye.

The noise louder, smellier... clinking, ringing... as she sat bolt upright, eyes alight. Ears tuning to the whispers of mice in the attic,

and there it was again... wafting... like Charlie's three-day old fish heads in the bin... the clink of metal on metal.

Darkness knew every nook and cranny in the old house as she hugged her pillow and tip toed to her brother's room and whispered... 'Charlie there's someone else in the house.' His nostril's guttural noise sounded a foul note for a moment, then resumed in ignorance. She twisted his earlobe, a reason he knew from his pestilence of past mischiefs, and he coughed aloud and groaned, 'Owe!' Her hand reached his mouth as she whispered again, 'There's someone in the house,' and breathed heavy in his ear, her scent filling his nostrils.

He shook his head again, 'Probably a cat,' his voice too loud.

The chill rattled by groans, filled the room, and washed in the air with moans of iron... It appeared... A patch so dark over one eye, all they saw was the bead of the other staring, a reflection deep in need.

With one hand, hat raised high he bowed like royalty, and them, the lords of this world.

'Ahh me hearty's,' arose so loud their teeth tightened, and in a voice so brazen they clasped in a frightened hug. 'You be the deeds of our undoing, so be warned. If the mistakes of our past are touched again, we will haunt those who were chosen by the crags of Pebble Rock and the ghost who bears its name... for he has broken the creed of Pirate Cove, and you will pay the price. You have until the next full moon turns to a quart slice of cheese. No less, no more, to return what was unearthly taken by one not worthy.'

He rattled his chains and drew his cutlass, and with one foul swipe he cut the darkness and disappeared.

'BANG-BANG,' as she opened the front door. 'What's up my

mum's at the shops,' Emily scratching her arm like it still pained her.

'Your parent's back from their holiday early?'

'No... we had a visitor last night,' Charlie rubbing his scar for courage.

'Charlie chickenshit, we were so scared, we were, and would have called, but you know we can't. So, we just sat scared frozen until the sun had fully risen.'

'Come on out with it what's got you so spooked, 'Emily's face contorted.

'A ghost, not our ghost, another, way scarier, and, and... he threatened us... he did... he did. Hanna's ribs paining with the pitch of her voice.

'Jack, that's who we need to ask, he's got all the dirt on what's going on around here. He'll know,' Charlie's scar finding away.'

'We can't use any mobiles. Just look what happened to the last two towers' they tried to erect. Up in smoke,' Emily pointing to the still burnt-out remnant on top of Medowville's highest hill. 'Tele mob reckoned on a "Sola Thing Me a Jig," that burnt out every internet transmitter for a hundred mile. Go-figure... but we know better, don't we,' Emily tapping her transistor radio to see if it still worked. 'We live in a stone age town. No wonder your parents wanted a holiday far away.'

'So where is Master Jack? Up to no good, I bet.' Hannah's folded arms matching her frown.

MR YELLOWFOOT'S shop was filled with the past, and once a month he made the hundred-mile journey for wares and every piece of nick-nacks a town like Medowville craved. He filled his lungs with the damp air and thought of what other wonders Yabba-yabba billabong might hold until a damp patch on his sock caught his attention.

    'Shoo, you awful dog,' shaking his foot. 'Jack, keep that mut of yours on a leash.'

    'Here, Bullseye. Sorry Mr Yellow.'

'Yellowfoot to you son, now where was I. Oh yes, Michael let me take another look at that mug you found.' He stared deep into the crystals dulled by age. 'Hand me that rag hanging by the clove spice rack young Jack.'

Jack looked back to see if Bullseye's knot was secure, his eyes scanning all the goods. Too many for most to know, but not for him, his hand reached the ragged rag, and he walked the ten feet to the counter, eyes full of, the jewel encrusted item.

One wipe with the worn rag and the sparkles sent the ancient mug into another universe, one where the jewels entered all their minds like diamonds in the sky. Mr Yellowfoot fumbled as his jeweller's eyepiece fell back to hand. His voice trembled, 'Where did you find this again?'

'I had to get permission of course it being a protected reserve and all from old Mrs Ritchie, what her being so poorly. It wasn't easy. Doo Duffle my dog, he was the one that found it. We went for the truffles, he has a nose for those, however pickings around here have been slim, but

Yabba-yabba billabong that's a whole nother world.' His face grey as he sucked in a large breath and said, 'Doo Duffle dropped it at my feet out there, part of a set I reckon, but that whole place gives me the creeps.'

In a worried voice, 'Who have you told?'

'Only my Mrs...Mavis...'

'Oh,' Mr Yellowfoot's hand covered his face to squash an expression. 'Jack here's a bag of gobstoppers, now not a word of this to anyone, you hear me, Jack. Not a word.'

'Cross me heart Mr Yellow,' as he stuffed one of the hard coated sweets into his mouth and sucked on the heavenly treat. 'Come on Bullseye,' his knot united with a spoiling spit.

TREEWARE held an irresistible attraction for Jack, with trinkets centuries old adorning the Willow-barks along with tales from the past, not to mention, the view it offered over Gossip Estuary. Jack's mind alight, like he was the wild colonial boy.

From behind, 'I told you...'as Bullseye's tail swirled with Charlie's hand stroking his patch right between his pure white ears.

'Rub my eyes and glue the soles of my feet to this rock... how did you lot find out,' his gobstopper nearly leaving his mouth.

'Find out what?' and three friends looked at each other.

'Come on Jack out with it, you know you can't keep it in, it's just who you are,' Emily's terse smile a dead giveaway.

'Least you could have let Bullseye dig up more of that treasure old man Flintoff's dog found. Hey Bullseye,' and he let the dog's saliva run like sap over the back of his hand. 'You boy can sniff out another dog's scent three days old,' as he scratched Bullseye under his chin avoiding a wet tongue kiss.

Together, 'Treasure... what treasure?'

'A jewel encrusted mug... buried I reckoned.'

'Buried was it, well we just had a visit from its owner,' Charlie's scar on fire like a prickly pear... 'And he wants it back before the moon turns to cheese.'

'No Charlie it's an old term meaning when the moon is nearly covered in darkness and the night is about to turn pitch black.' Hannah explaining every detail to Jack's stare, and when she was finished his gobstopper was swallowed whole, unable to talk.

'What do we do, we don't want to get haunted for the rest of our lives, and what other terrible things might...' Emily's voice cracking...

Hannah's arm settling on hers... 'Don't worry we'll find a way...together...That's what we do, right everyone?'

'We better be quick, because Old Man Flintoff told his Mrs, and we all know what that means.'

Hannah frowned, 'Every dog, child, man, woman and insect will soon be out looking for that treasure. What can-'

'Stop... We have to, contact him... even though we breach his code... the code of The Ghost of Pebble Rock.'

'It is not that time of year yet Charlie?'

'But we must, surely,' Charlie voice echoing in their every thought... Charlie scratching his head, 'How long until the moon is gone, and darkness descends?'

'A week, may-be less, according to Mick MacCoy the only fisherman I trust with my Mackerel,' Jack sucking on his third gobstopper.

'Come, we have to go now,' Charlie running over the one and only rickety bridge to their ghost's home amongst the swamp.

Three wallabies and a toad sat waiting for treats. 'Sorry,' Hannah puffed as she passed. 'Next time, we are on a mission to save us all,' and she gulped.

'How can we wake him up, this being six weeks from the one day a year he appears to us,' Emily's breathing laboured into a bare whisper. 'Stop I can't keep up,' exhausted she flopped bent over gasping for breath.

'Stop Charlie she's right... Can we even wake him,' Hannah distressed.

'Look ahead, through the mist of the swamp. What do you see,' Charlie pointed.

'A whole lot of nothing, but the Craggie Cliff, that surrounds his swamp. He normally sends a message to show the way, so we don't fall foul of the bog, but not this time... Nothing,' Emily gasped.

'I'm going to climb one of those Craggs and jump,' Charlie feeling his scar for luck.

'You're crazy, you are going to go splat on some rock, or submerged tree stump,' Jack spitting his gobstopper at the thought.

'Crazy is what crazy does. We are all crazy trusting our lives to a ghost for protection,' and he felt his scar again,' but I can't explain, I just know I have to try.'

Two frogs and three frilled lizards and a porcupine looked up at the stranger climbing the craggiest peak as Charlie emerged from within the fog.

'There,' Emily pointed. The whispers from toads and crickets hushed to a silence as a lizard and joey stared up as if they knew.

Charlie edged further out on the ledge that hung like a diving platform without a pool.

'I can't look,' Hannah turning to Emily, for words meant nothing and they hugged, for comfort.

Charlie looked out over the mist to the golden rays of a setting sun and held out his hand in hope.

'He's gone,' Jack blurted.

Deafly silence befell, not one cricket, dare a sound. They heard no splash, not even a squeak.

'You could have stopped him,' Jack frowned. 'No, we all should have stopped him,' he stammered. 'Gone is he... Gone forever.'

***

Pirates Ahoy me hearty's

The gravel of sensibility washed into the sea-salt of voice as he awoke, but the voice unforgettable, as he heard...

'This place, our place, time is a mistress... and our past, the future young Charlie.

We live in a bubble, tied by heritage and location.

You feel it, don't you...

A need some call greed, some call providence, but I call it instincts...

The nose on your face...

The smell of desire...

a reason to belong, stirred by feelings in the pit of your stomach, driving your brain to the wheelhouse on my four posted Spanish Galleon... A square rigger, with a heart... me hearty... Ha, ha... snakes alive, your alive young Charlie.

Charlie shook his head, pounding to the race of his heart and looked up. The face of his ghost no longer showed the splits of wood carved into craggy features. Eyes no more the round markings gestured by the strike of butterfly wings with the worm of his tongue swallowed... by his pure human youthfulness... A pink scar ran down the length of one cheek and broadened as he said.

'You are in my time, where serpents sweep the seas and a pirate's greed is an open chest of jewels to secure a future. So welcome aboard,' and he held out his hand. Rough texture lifted Charlie to his feet, and Charlie felt his hand tingle for a second. 'Sorry son, the ropes of my ship bind my grip into brazen calluses of hope.

A creak on the deck behind them made them turn.

'Our second in command Charlie.'

The salt air thick with tongue, 'Cap, a merchant schooner ten miles to starboard,' his voice young, like he imagined himself in five or so years.

'All hands, on deck,' a real ghost bellowed, sharpened by youthful expertise.

And where there were three, twenty appeared, as if the knots in the wood had secrets...

And they all stared... at him... a boy without a clue.

'No time for introductions. Raise the Jolly Roger and get that forestay trim and tight me hearties. Up the rigging lads... She's no slouch that spice trader. Just look at her wake... and I guess a pretty penny on board.

With narrow of eye and sharpened voice he uncorked a rope from the masthead and reached one arm around Charlie's waist... together they swung across a rolling deck to the wheelhouse steps. 'Best you stay below son when the action erupts,' and he lowered a patch over one eye. 'Blind men see in the dark when they cover one eye,' and he smiled, all but one tooth perfect

The crisp of wood on wood echoed from within a hatch made door. 'Down here sonny,' his wooden peg leg leading the way. 'I'm Broth the cook... boy, but if the lads need another blade,' and he twirled the dull metal, more knife than sword, and placed it back between his teeth as they climbed down a second flight of stairs.

'The bilge, boy. Where all good cooks, stores their treasures. Just smell the ripeness of this tomato. Don't mind the worms, they give the grub a true sense of impunity.'

Charlie shook his head again... for answers were but grains of sands washed in an ocean of the unknown... and Broth here smelt unlikely, just like his supper

***
.

'Test the boundaries one more time Jack,' Hannah muddy head to toe.

'Useless it is, useless.' Jack spat as he wiped both eyes like wipers on a car that had extracted itself from the torture of black peat.

'Here... use my scarf, Jack,' Emily untying the waist cloth allowing her dress to flower.

'Worst still, the snakes, and I don't know what that beast is with the scales, but when he opens his mouth... I hate to think what's next.'

'Did you see the swirl in the bog, sure to suck us down even if we could breach the perimeter,' Jack's face near on unrecognizable as he handed the dress tie back dripping in filth.

'No, you might need it again,' her smirk almost funny but she knew it wasn't.

'Come on, we have to climb up for a better look just like...' and a tear filled her eye for in her heart she knew her brother was gone.

So, they climbed, and halfway Jack stopped, ears pricked to a familiar bark.

'It's Bullseye,' eyes straining in-between a sunset and dusk as he saw a trail of lanterns centipede the rickety old bridge.

Bullseye's bark drifted between each breath of breeze. 'They've untied him,' Jacks voice cracked... 'He'll find us for sure.'

'The secrets out and they all want a piece,' Emily one hand on a craggy ledge the other pointing.

A yelp and a groan, was it? Far off cries of 'Catch that,' disappeared in the mist with the flickers of light heading their way, and they paused, confused, silent... until... out of the mist a leathery wet tongue found his master.

'Bullseye,' lead bitten through, and with one lick, eyes wide he stared deep into his owner's big blue ones, and barked as if he knew what he should do.

He yelped again with front paws gripping every rock ledge as he climbed higher... Up, up he went until all they saw was the tips of his white ears.

'Come back Bullseye... Stop!' Jack yelled as they all followed, lost in a world not of their making.

... With two girls tied into the desperate confusion... Higher, higher, until they all reached the top. On the edge Bullseye teetered and looked back one last time and barked just once. The black spot between his jet white ears disappeared as Jack's word of 'No,' meant nothing as the edge swallowed Bullseye and Jack looked down.

The mist swirled for a second as if it knew, but still ate his pal, the one thing, he loved more than life itself. 'No,' he cried again, and if tears were a young boy's soul, he let out a renewed insanity.

Face stripped by tears, 'Just like Bullseye,' he choked once again and swallowed, 'I saw,' and spluttered 'This whirlpool of mist devoured my best friend,' and with the words of her brother on his lips he disappeared into the depths of the bottomless fog... Down, down, he went with the pull etching into the young girl's minds.

They looked down to the

lanterns of town folk nearing the bog below, and as they stared deep into each other's eyes, they held hands, for the loneliness of belonging in this world was too much to bear, without the feelings they shared for the others...

And... they stepped out, into the fog of the future... or was it the past?

'PICKLE THE STEW, what have we here?' Broth side stepping two girls spread eagled on the "Poop Deck."

Emily opened one eye, the other stuck fast with mud. 'Oh,' she groaned as Hannah gasped, and before they could move a wet rough tongue washed their faces in saliva.

From way up high, rope in hand, a pirate swung. He was young, a half-grown moustache hardly noticeable and below his head scarf, flowing black hair swirled.

'You came,' his face surprised.

Hannah looked at Emily as they grabbed each other's hands, trying to stand, and together they said, 'Charlie?'

'Shh,' Broth spoke in a mumble barely above the wind. 'We have to hide you two lovelies away... The spirits of the sea will not be happy...

bad luck,' he grumbled. 'Follow me,' treading like the boards had ears... and down the steps into the captain's cabin, but alas the rigging had already spied, and he could hear their whispers spreading from yard arm to crow's nest.

'Captain look who we found on our beloved "Poop Deck."'

'Welcome aboard, me lovelies,' he smiled... and from behind a door a well-dressed pirate laughed... 'Told you, didn't I,' Jack smiled, then lowered his eyes as he caught the captain's frown. We will have to

Confused the girls looked at each other and then to Jack who seemed remarkably refreshed given they were a mere minute or so behind him...

And before they could offer a word the captain whistled a tune, they had all heard before, in another time, another place... and they stared at him... so handsome, so young, surely not the ghost they knew so well, and when he stopped to lick his lips he said,

'Every minute that passes in your time is a day here. How many has it been Charlie?

"I don't know, a year or two. I lose track, to be honest.'

'Half nearly a man, aren't you, but you two girls are a pirate's captain's nightmare, for the folk law of the fairer sex on ships tend to tear at the crew's demon thoughts... We will have to show them who we really are... Isn't that right Charlie.'

'Charlie smiled, 'Right,' and with that a knock on the captain's door interrupted

'Bedlam, what can we do for you,' the first mate's knife quiet in its scabbed.

'The crew have questions, and need answers,' behind twenty eyes strained for a view of the girls.

'Hannah and Emily, you best hold your breaths because things are going to a little weird as this being your first time,' and his pink scar broadened as if it knew.

They followed the request because trust is a very precious thing.

All about swirled in confusion as if they could see straight through to the souls of the crew, and when they released their breath Charlie had vanished, in front of their eyes.

'Where for art though Charlie,' their ghost asked, and Bedlam raised his right arm as if rehearsed.

His captain (their ghost) clipped Bedlam across the ears knocking him senseless to the floor and without a word Charlie's ghostly body stood erect and he breathed out... as real as the boy they knew, only older, almost unrecognisable.

Bedlam's still body however lay on the floor unconscious... Charlie turned to the remaining crew and said...

'Boo!'

Horror breathed within the voices of the crew like stories of giant squid eating pirate ships... with the whispers of "ghost girls" placed between mermaids and the captain's threat...

'Mess with them me hearty's and you'll walk the plank to Davy Jone's locker... or... with luck... You might end up with the insight of me first mate Bedlam here,' and as their captain raised his fingers Bedlam's matted hair waved to his touch like scared pilchard on an orca's run...

'Come girls,' as they breathed out and pinched each other just to be sure, for sure...as their captain said in a stern voice, 'We have a prophecy to create.

In the beginning

Blue sparkles and purple bubbles wafted about to explode, as heady tunes of three blind mice cleared.

. Foggy he saw adjacent, strung by a right leg, a trapeze artist.

'Broke me leg,' a boy

, about his age said.

'Couldn't have happened to a nicer person,' a girl's voice He looked out; room full of three other children.

'You're awake at last.'

'What happened?' Charlie confused.

'Bus crash,' her arm in a plaster, cast from shoulder to wrist.

He tried to lift his head off the pillow, but it appeared to belong to another, not him as it bled into his stiff white sheets.

His head, cotton balls bound by spider white bandages, wound too tight.

'No don't move,' he heard, 'they said to ring the bell if you wake and say don't move your head. Something might be broke.'

He lifted his hand... nose, eyes, mouth... for he knew his head was in there, somewhere.

'Bandages bud. We all have them,' Trapeze boy swinging to a sitting position.

'That's Jack, and you know who I am, don't you?'

Her voice washed in the fog of yesteryear, and he tried for a glimpse, a dimple of hope shattered by shards of regret.

'It's Hannah... Your twin?'

'Oh, ah...yea... Hannah.'

'On your other side is Emily, she broke her funny bone.'

'No jokes, even humerus,' and everyone laughed.

'Please, please don't make me laugh, these fractured ribs break my heart,' Hannah moaned.

'That means we have something in common.' Emily looking from bandages to plaster, and a large metal frame with five toes ready for a good scratching. 'Leg, arm, rib and broken crown to call our own, and when we meet out of this place, all we have to do is rub the pain away with the memory of experience.'

'Not the sort of experience we want to remember, but we could be friends,' Hannah said.

'Like mates,' Jack licking the end of his desert fork and magically disappearing it into the top of his leg plaster.

'Who wants to be mates with a girl,' Charlie's head feeling more like it belonged.

'Charlie, fiddlesticks. Don't listen to my brother, Emily. If you want to be mates, then we are mates... Right Charlie?'

His head hurt again, 'Right,' he said... and just when he thought it couldn't get any worse, the room door opened. Mist poured in like the fog of an early morning's broken dawn, only this was ten, not five am.

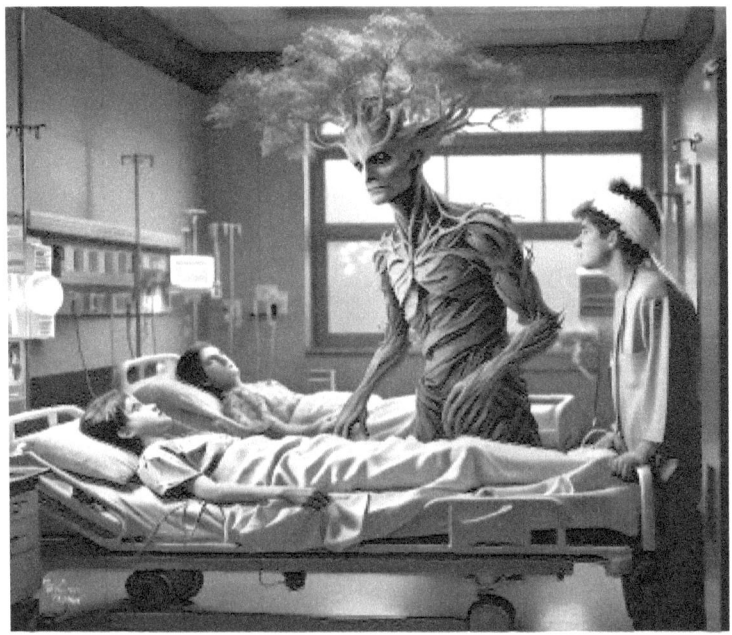

'Womm ... womm,' came echoing out until the sound filled every corner. The long snake of an instrument moved within their midst. 'Womm, womm, wom!' Until it snapped solid, a long slim barrel etched with ancient carvings crawling with the thickened taste of swamp toad... and they saw him... Tall, a weathered tree with cracks opening for a face, a worm or two would enjoy. So wooden he might break as he moved closer, they thought.

'Fee five foe one, I smell the scent of frightened ones', and he stepped in solid, like an oak.

He must be Captain Starlight I've heard the nurses talk of,' Hannah whispered through Jack's bandages.

'Who might you be, little Missy?' his voice like splitting timber.

'Me? Why Hannah,' trying to be brave in spite of her aching heart, as she stepped behind Jacks bed, just to be safe.

'I know who you are,' Emily said. 'You're the entertainment for us sick kids.'

'Entertainment, ha, ha, ha,' like a forest alive... 'I'm here, to point the way,' he rustled and looked at Charlie like he should know, but Charlie didn't have a clue.

'Point the way,' Hannah asked.

'Follow the clues, follow the clues,' he creaked and without a whisper the mist grew thick, so thick, Jack swore he could write his name mid-air, and without a trace Captain Starlight had vanished.

'Well, that's one hell of an act,' Emily said.

'Sure is,' Hannah replied and with her words barely out her mouth, the door swung open, and a nurse entered, pushing a pill trolley.

'Phew, this place tastes like a damp dirty dungeon. Let me open a window and let some fresh air in,' with a creak and a snap she sucked in a deep breath. 'Isn't that better?'

'We really enjoyed the show,' Jack said. 'So convincing, your Captain Starlight and his vanishing act. He had us all going.'

'Oh, so I see you're awake, at last,' she said. 'What's this about Captain Starlight, sorry son but the entertainment is only on Tuesdays and Fridays, and today is Monday. That wack on the head has you seeing things.'

'But we all saw him Sister,' Emily said. 'Tall, arms and legs like tree trunks, playing some musical pipe... and his face, a face so cracked it looked like it would break. We all saw him.'

The nurse turned and glared at each child for a moment, and muttered to herself, before walking to look out the open window and taste the scent of eucalyptus. 'You know I just came from the bus driver, who's recovering well, just so you know, and he said... No, I shouldn't...' she breathed in deep to clear a thought, 'he said, no he swore, the reason for the crash... get this... A mist came from nowhere, and this chap just planted himself fair in the middle of the road, unavoidable, and... the whole bus just filled with this strange music as real as a didgeridoo, but don't tell anyone because the doctors think he's crazy, and she smiled and sung 'crazy, crazy, crazy,' as she went to fetch the doctor for Jack.

Hannah looked at Jack as he stared at Emily, and Emily at Charlie, with no one game to say the words they were all thinking... "Ghost of pebble rock."

Six weeks passed...

'Tread carefully with those crutches Jack,' Emily side stepping two sharp rocks.

'The doc said another week and I can throw them away,' as he pushed the thick brush aside, signs of a track long vanished.

Ahead native plants broke open to a clearing of wild grasses and moss rocks.

'Town folk reckon a spirit lives here and have a name for the place, Yabba Yabber Billabong.'

'Jack Small, I just love the bush,' Hannah smiled and sucked in the scrub's earthy flavour, ribs settling to a scratching ache. 'What do you think happened to the first people of this land?'

'I hate to think,' and he brushed off the flower of bottlebrush from his shirt. 'Tell us Charlie, this fascination with old man Richie.'

'He's a nice elderly man Jack,' Emily stretching her fingers, fresh from the confines of plaster. 'Pity his wife has taken so ill, I hear he spends all his waking hours on her care, so mum says.'

Jack lay down his crutches and sat on the largest moss rock. 'My dad reckons this place is worth a mint. We passed all those dozers and heavy diggers on our way here, didn't we?'

'The rickety old bridge over Gossip Creek wouldn't support one of them,' Emily said seating herself next to Hannah with Charlie walking in circles, searching. 'Sandwich anyone?'

'To early,' Jack licking his finger and dabbing a raw spot on his leg. 'Those trucks aren't there for nothing. My dad is friends with turdy Tanner of Tanner's Realty. Reckons they're going to build a new bridge over Gossip Estuary. What do you think is going to happen to our Silver Swamp? Old man Richie owns the lot.'

'I'll have a sandwich,' Hannah's stomach rumbling to the taste of an empty burp.

'They have plans,' Jack continued. 'A golf course, houses, canals and get this...' arms stretched, a wedgetail eagle would envy... 'One grandiose yacht club. That's what.'

'Do you think Mr Richie will sell?' and out of the bush a little scrub wallaby hoped.

'Oh, how cute,' Emily breaking off a piece of her sandwich and tossing.

'Beautiful,' Hannah seeing the mother hiding three banksias back. Hesitant, her joey's ears pricked before nibling a piece, only to stop and stare, at the strangers in a baby's home.

'I have it,' Charlie pulling a map from his pocket. Everyone looked as he brushed the moss from a rock. 'Which way do you think the arrow points?' and again brushed the rock with his foot.

'That's not much of an arrow, looks more like a squashed toad with a flattened head.'

'Oh Jack, look passed the green stuff. Old man Richie,' and he saw his sister's nose wrinkle. He paused and looked down. 'Mr Richie said this map is the key to a buried treasure in our Silver Swamp. The reason he bought the property in the first place, he said... that and his wife fell in love with the area.' Charlie stopped and turned to Hannah. 'Mr Richie shook, and his voice cracked when he explained how he and his wife spent half their life searching for the treasure. He told of tales from old timers, their eyes like saucers as they described jewels the size of golf balls, and a pirate's cove. All he found was lizards, frogs, a tortoise or two and a whole lot of mud. The map, useless as his blasted compass in the swamp. It points the way all righty, but in the end, there is no destination marked, only twenty hectares of marsh to frustrate a sane man. Maybe you will have more luck sonny he said, and left handing me the map singing... crazy, crazy, crazy, stupid map.'

'Is that a silver back tortoise?' Hannah pointed. 'Looks like he knows the way,' and they followed, before... look at all those frilled lizards flaring... almost flags to a sailor, don't you think?'

'A pirate maybe,' Jack laughed. 'What do they say about girls on a ship?' Charlie about to answer when he saw a flared screwed nose.

'A sign maybe,' Hannah pulling a twig from her shoe. 'What does the map say?'

Charlie lay the map down for all to see as the black cloth swirled like he'd soaked it in vinegar.

'Ruined. You must have let your drink spill all over that old piece of ink,' Jack kicking a root too thick and bellowed 'Ah, oh, bite my bum,' and dropped both crutches to sink defeated.

'It's all my fault, I'm sorry,' and Charlie's scar throbbed with his fingers pressing trying to stop the pain.

'Don't worry Charlie,' Emily's touch tender on his scar, halving the despair, and he looked up, to brave for a tear. 'No wait look' she said, and the black ink swirled to a cross, and a path to show the way.

'Well, I'll be a Kentucky Fried Vegan,' Jack blurted to lift a crutch, attention drawn to a sudden movement next to his right foot. A creatures head the size of a half-grown croc, slithered, snake eyes of underripe tomatoes, and the forked tongue to make Jack forget his crutches.

Womm, womm, womm echoed alive, all about, and the bush grew damp. A mist so thick they all huddled together. Unseen the magic, too late for escape. No path but in front, snake eyes behind, and they walked like little lost sheep guided by the venom of future's past.

Distant, Pebble Rock shone, a beacon to see by, but ahead the track disappeared, swallowed by swamp things...alive they moved and out of the mist he strode, their ghost... With a voice of grinding timber, he rose again on the back of a Spanish Galleon, a tattered Jolly Roger around his neck. 'You know Charlie what it means to be alive, young thing. You found the way,' he breathed, and with a wooden foot he kicked open the pirate's chest of jewels. Ablaze in the beams from pebble rock they shone. 'Now you know the task ahead young Charlie.'

Charlie shook his head, 'Who are you, what task?'

'To save all you taste, smell and hear. All that surrounds,' and he grasped tight his long wooden pipe.

Charlie's face whitened, 'You're the ghost with the magic?' and he rubbed his scar as if for a clue.

Thick with moisture he spat, 'How can I achieve such goals. I'm just a legend, but you Charlie, you are the one to show the way.'

'Me, why me?'

'My time is short, and you have much. I'm a mere reflection of what makes this place alive, the past, the present and you Charlie, the future.' He lifted his pipe and blew, "womm womm womm..." 'Take a look, the creatures, the plants.' Sounds and smells so sweet Charlie could taste their need. 'Will we survive,' he croaked, 'or die? Brim and firestorm have no place here, I am the ingredients of all you see. No match for the machinery of man, and when they finish, I'll simply be crushed black dirt blowing in the dust of their deals,' and out of the mouth of a friend...

'The jewels. Old man Richie's treasure. He'll never sell if he can afford to care for his missus. Probably make a reserve out of this place, knowing him.'

'Young Jack your leg is strong and mind rich with an answer. Take what you need and make the deals that creates the future.'

Three weeks passed... Mrs Richie waited...

'My chair has wheels of fortune and you Charlie, my love,' and she cried a tear of embrace that slid down her cheek. Brave for a second, he kneeled and let her touch heal his scar, with the salt of his tears mixing into the joy of hers.

The town could never fathom why the bridge over Gossip Swamp was not built, and a plaque to the Buccaneer, Black Ben, erected at the entrance of Silver Swamp... But once a year, four friends celebrate, in a wild rocky swamp, thick with wildlife and sing the tribute song, to the ghost of pebble rock...***

The Word is Believe

The ship drifted, becalmed, sails dewdrops of lilt and with a lacklustre of guilt on his face he said, 'I look into your eyes soiled by questions so big they leave me in despair,' and he breathed out, stripped by wishes with few answers... 'So, take heart, me young ones, they will come with the hardship of the journey ahead.

Call up the breeze lads and sing the pirate song out loud, because we "aint" got all day to catch that scurvy crew ahead. I can smell their black hearts trembling right now... Ho, Ho and a bottle of rum. Come on sing it out loud... You to young ones because where we're going "aint" no can of treats,' and he felt his scar near healed on his cheek.

And as they sang the spirit of the sea air heard their soulful request and breathed out.

'See me hearties, all you have to do is ask rightly of our mistress and she shall grant.' The sails filled, half trimmed balloons topped by a skull and crossbones. "Heave Ho, Heave Ho" they sang, and their wake spread out like only a pirate Galleon on a ghostly mission had a right to summon.

'Charlie, show us again the way to hold a sword,' and he smiled... 'Like this,' and as he swung, he near decapitated Bullseye. With a yelp the dog jumped into Jack's safe waiting arms.

'Charlie careful.'

'Sorry,' Charlie puffed. 'It's more like our ghostly Captain explained... All we have to do is, train our bodies to hold our breath for 3 minutes... That should be enough to enter the bodies of the other pirate ship's crew and their experience will imprint on us.' With eyes wide, 'sword play will be but a formality.'

'How does it feel,' Hannah's face contorted, 'You know, when you are on the inside,' and she looked at Charlie like he was the ghost with the knowledge.

Charlie smiled, 'You are still you... but you see through their eyes, and whatever skills they have are yours to take while in there and...' he stared deep into Emily's eyes, ' We control their will like they are our captives, but be warned, choose carefully the skill because wicked is the devil of the deed and will be lost to them once you leave.' Charlie looked to Bullseye and twirled the sword into the air, a toy within his hand, controlled like a musician with a lifeful of experience,' and he smiled, teeth perfect. He lowered his voice, 'Bedlam hides within the cabin's nowadays, missing two toes and a finger, for he has lost all expertise with anything sharp

As he spoke their Captain redirected his attention from the prey ahead to them. 'Youngins this is the time to create a presence. We... I mean you, are gifted with abilities that scares the pants of mere mortal men,' and he looked at the girls... 'and women. So, here's what we do. When the pitchforks are in the fire, you control the deeds to your home world, and mine. Always remember that. Without us, all you love and hold dear will be gone,' and his face grew grey... 'So, take the instructions I have given you, with faith, and he turned away...

The spice-trader a mere hundred metres ahead, as they trailed her like a rat on a piece of meat... for the use of cannons as a broadside risked the treasure he needed.

The bang splintered the wood and shredded the bottoms of sails...

'Blast,' he exploded, they have a Demi-Culverin swivel gun. Take cover young-ins we will have to decommission that pig of a nuisance first,' and as they ducked below the wheel house Emily didn't move, whimpering, in shock.

'Emily... Captain her leg,' Hanna yelled.

Crouching, 'I'll get her,' Charlie cried, and as he picked her up, blood streamed from her left calf. 'She's hit,' he yelled.

'Be quick, the reload of that menace is a mere two minutes... Charros, prepare the ropes we're boarding, and Jack tie a torniquet around Emily's leg. We don't want her bleeding out while we're away,' and he looked at their faces, shading from white to grey. I know the first time in combat is hard, but this is where legends are born and we are already one down, and out of time... Wait, wait,' he yelled as the next volley of lead exploded over their heads., 'Grab the ropes lads and young-ins... see the three on the bridge... the one with the red scarf is the captain, the yellow his second in command, and Jack, the wheel man is all yours. You take them out and all the others will falter,' and he gulped. 'Just give us a minute to silence that gun,' and he lowered the eye patch over his left eye. 'Pirates can see below decks with this, hey me hearties... All aboard,' and they swung as waves crashed the stern of the spice trader into their bow.

Swords and knives gleamed in the open air as the Demi Culverin was silenced... and on a breath of hot wind they heard... 'Swing now young-ins, and hold your breaths, least you be dead.'

With slide of feet a spice captains pleasure's entered Charlie's mind, of which he knew none of, so he turned to the experiences of leadership this spice captain held...for... he was already a dab hand with a sword... but before he was about to breath out he kept a promise and ordered... 'Throw down your weapons men,' and as he breathed out he stepped to one side as their captain fell to the deck... And appeared in front of them as large as life.

Beside him Hanna and Jack appeared. All who saw gasped, for moments, can take forever when the unbelievable is first seen

...But then, a rumbling from a man twice Charlie's size... his face full of fury as he stepped forward, sword pointing.

'Aye Roger Jefferies,' Charlie said. 'You are, as I recall, the rough tough child, pick pocket, who stole my trinkets before we indentured you to me... Isn't that, right?'

A puzzled look becalmed his savage face... 'What trickery is this...'

As another voice amongst the chaos echoed... 'Devil.'

'Will Smithers you aint no saint... We saved you from the hangman's noose... not true?'

Charlie's question interrupted from below decks, from a real pirate captain, and as he emerged, he announced... 'Lay down your weapon's everyone, for we command all below and wish no further bloodshed... Hey me hearties... and his crew "young ins included," cheered... for the scent of passion of the spice traders, had lost the heart of the fight...

Their captain... sprawled helpless in front of them, rubbing his head nonsensical.

'Charlie, you take command of my ship, while I'll keep a handful of our lads to mind their p's and q's here,' and he closed his right eye and whistled the tune of success,' before... 'Jack how's your skill as a wheelman now?'

'Just give me a direction, Jack replied. 'North, south, east or west, and I'll have her bowsprit splitting the centre.'

'Spoken like a diehard wheelman young Jack.,' and from his pocket he pulled a metal case and opened it. 'Follow the pointer and point her nose to windward.'

Jack held the compass and looked down... A skull and crossbones on the dial had an arrow turning towards it, as he spun the ships wheel one more time.

'What skills may I ask have you acquired young Hanna,' a question only a ghost with a past could say.

Without a word she grasped a wet rope and swung back aboard the Black Bounty like a cat tip toeing on the wet patches of spray... Almost forgotten she turned to see Emily, a bandana strapped leg half hopping to embrace her as she mumbled 'What's next?' and almost smiled as they heard…

'Charlie, time for a captain to have a ship. The Black Bounty is all yours…' Charlie's eyes wide… 'Take her and the crew and follow us… Right Jack.'

'Aye captain,' Jack's face broadened with joy, for he was only missing one thing. A dog barked too afraid to jump between the two sailing ships.

'Here let me,' Hanna chirped as she whisked Bullseye up like a mop on the end of her rope. He squirmed and yelped at Jack's feet, and all they saw was the back of her flaming red hair in the wind.

Queen of the Banshees

Emily yelled instructions to Charlie, grateful for any help, for they had entered the Tigerless Straits. Jack looked down, the skull and crossbones on his dial had the arrow turning towards the Jolly Roger insignia as he spun the ships wheel one more time.

'Point her nose to windward and follow the arrow,' he heard.

Either side, ships submerged masts rising from the jagged rocks like serpent's teeth trying for a bite... and with a gust of wind they heard the banshee scream.

'Hard to starboard,' Emily yelled as Jack wrestled.

'Helm's, like a pig in a vice,' he muttered.

'Steady as she goes,' his captain's eye glued to a telescope, and for a second he thought he saw the splash of silver tail protruding from a piece of reef.

From nowhere they were swallowed... Mist so thick all went white... Silence befell as Charlie's ears pricked to the whispers of Emily's voice through the fog... Out of the damp a stream of sunshine shone, a beacon, for whatever was hidden by the fog, the banshee's voices, ever closer.

Out of the white they appeared, sails dragging limp and before they had a chance to toss anchors their bows rode up upon the sandy white shore... aground.

They looked up to the craggy cliffs above and unbeknown to them their ghost had left his heart to another.

She called out, and all who heard shuddered with the ripples of her voice caught in the time-pool of this place.

'Over the side young ins. We are off to see her Majesty,' and a tear filled his eye... quickly wiped for he knew time was running out.

Up they climbed, the rugged trail lined by spiky plants prickling their senses... Emily studied Charlie ahead... 'Age becomes you Charlie,' and deep inside she could feel the changes in how she looked at him, with feelings so vivid, she blushed, because she too had been in this place to long.

The track stopped at a set of sculptured steps. Weary they gazed upwards to glimpse an elegant balcony peaking its nose outwards... With every step the purple marble revealed more... Grand sculptures blended, ten times the size of a man... at the centre ... a statue of a majestic woman, hair entwined by sleeping silent sea snakes... waiting.

Below the squeals from Banshee's boiled the water as if they were awakening a queen. Deep inside the cavernous cathedral four red eyes growled, and if by magic she appeared... the statue no match for her glistening beauty.

'Silence dogs,' and they stepped back into the black as she let out a scorching screech and all about fell deftly quiet. 'Hermoids, it has been too long,' and their captain stepped forward.

'Yes, my...' and his words dried up to... 'I know.'

Her voice cracked to break the whistle in her tune,' as she said. 'What little creatures have we here,' and as she smiled, they saw her razor-sharp teeth no knife could match.

'A promise for the future,' he said. Step forward young ins, and hold Bullseye put, least he be ripped to shreds.'

'Let me take a look... who hold much promise,' and she drew in a large nasal breath, and looked to the heavens... the clouds parted... as if she was their mistress. Forward she stepped, Life is a journey... we don't know the reasons, we don't know the story, but you little ones hold the future in your hands... So, hold them out and let me see. Palm up or how else can I predict... are you... can you... grow flowers in the heart of your needs,' and she stared past them to their captain, the ghost of Pebble Rock and said, 'Greed is a tempting mistress... at first just a note of desire, but in time, ah time, it takes the irk of a wish and transforms into our every thought... friendships, families,' and she looked her Hermoids (their captain)... 'loved ones cast to the wind, for what, the glimmer... No... the power... of riches, jewels to our flaws.' Her voice rasped by a break in her heart, and she clasped her chest... A heartbeat no human can hear... except for those so chosen, and they all felt her pain, even their ghost... and he turned away.

'What can we do,' Charlie said?

Her eyes ablaze, like he had challenged her.

She calmed herself and said, 'There is a great undoing happening in your time... but with the grace of nature's long past,' and she looked to the heavens. 'You are protected by an unearthly event buried in the very soul of our earth... where even the wizardry of mankind, can't touch. Their inventions useless in your Yabba-Yabba billabong and its surrounds.' She held Charlie's hand, 'Your ghost, my Hermoids, must pass on his pirate's decree, on to one who awaits your return. For there is much danger coming for those that are chosen... but important are you, because you have a chance to undo what is done.' She sighed, For the inventions that outstep the boundaries of nature, will surely be but toppings, to a hungry universe,' and her look made Bullseye whimper.

'The trader's ship is pilled full for the journey as you requested,' their captain said.

'Cinamon from Sri Lanka,
Nutmeg from Jamaca,

Tea from Ceylon
Garlic from Pakistan,
And ginger from India...
And I shall bid you farewell young ins.'
'You are not coming,' Hanna said?
'No there is another,' and he paused, 'More worthy.'
'But we love the smell of heather on the rough texture of your bark. The way you command the sense of charcoal breaking in the morning in Yabba-Yabba billabong,' and he smiled all but one tooth perfect.

'The meaning of all you have learnt here, will always be with you, but the skill will leave your bodies. But, if needs are strong, you can develop them again. It is for you to decide. Whatever happens from this day forth is your destiny, so choose wisely. Off to the spice trader young ins... Fair winds me hearties and I will see you in the great beyond,' and he held out his hand as they clambered down and they all turned one last time to see him turn to another, the queen of the Banshees with his palm up.

'Take the wheel Jack, and men... To the sails.'

'Aye captain Charlie,' for they all knew that a banshee hung on his every order, ready to devour should they disobey.

Above the heavens opened as a full tide swung their bow seawards into the future.

'What happened,' Emily groggy? At her feet a tattered skull and crossbones... with the others shaking their heads trying to stand...

All about powdery remnants of skeletons dressed in threads of clothes. Jack lifted a cap with the tip of his sword, 'Isn't that...' his face grew young to a childish 'Yikes.'

'Look at me twelve again,' Charlie said, 'And the crew just rags to ashes.'

'Time hasn't aged them well,' Hanna said with an almost childish smirk as Bullseye licked her hand.

On the deck of the Black-Bounty they smelt the damp taste of masts eaten through by wood rot. Her deck all but holding their weight as they looked out to a swamp infested with bities.

From afar a young woman's cry. 'A miracle,' Emily pointed. They followed her finger... At the end a beautiful black haired young woman planted a foot on a serpent's head, and with a flick of its tail she surfed across the mud splattered filth.

'Who are you,' Charlie asked?

'I'm... I'm...' unable to answer.

'Look at her ring finger Charlie,' Hanna said.

'It can't be,' Charlie stared in disbelief.

'It's old man Richie's Mrs, she's reincarcerated.'

'It's reincarnated Jack, but she looks exactly like her wedding photo I once saw. So young. She hasn't aged a day.' and Emily smiled.

'I don't know where I am, I don't know who I am,' she said... 'but I do know I must protect all about including you,' and she smiled in an almost ghostly glow, and they all held their breaths... for the ghosts of Pebble Rock... had no mercy for those who wanted its destruction.

The End.

IF YOU ENJOYED THIS story, we would love a like and a review.

Other books by us
The Last Dragon's egg
All the Kings horses

Don't miss out!

Visit the website below and you can sign up to receive emails whenever Brian Dry publishes a new book. There's no charge and no obligation.

https://books2read.com/r/B-A-OHTK-AFMHE

BOOKS 2 READ

Connecting independent readers to independent writers.

Also by Brian Dry

The Last Dragon's egg
Ghost of Pebble Rock
Pirates Ahoy (Ghost of Pebble Rock)